Hettie **loved** hats: tall hats, small hats, any size at all hats, round hats, pointy hats, fancy hoity toity hats.

MY
S!

Written
Tracy Gun

Illustrated by
Alea Marley

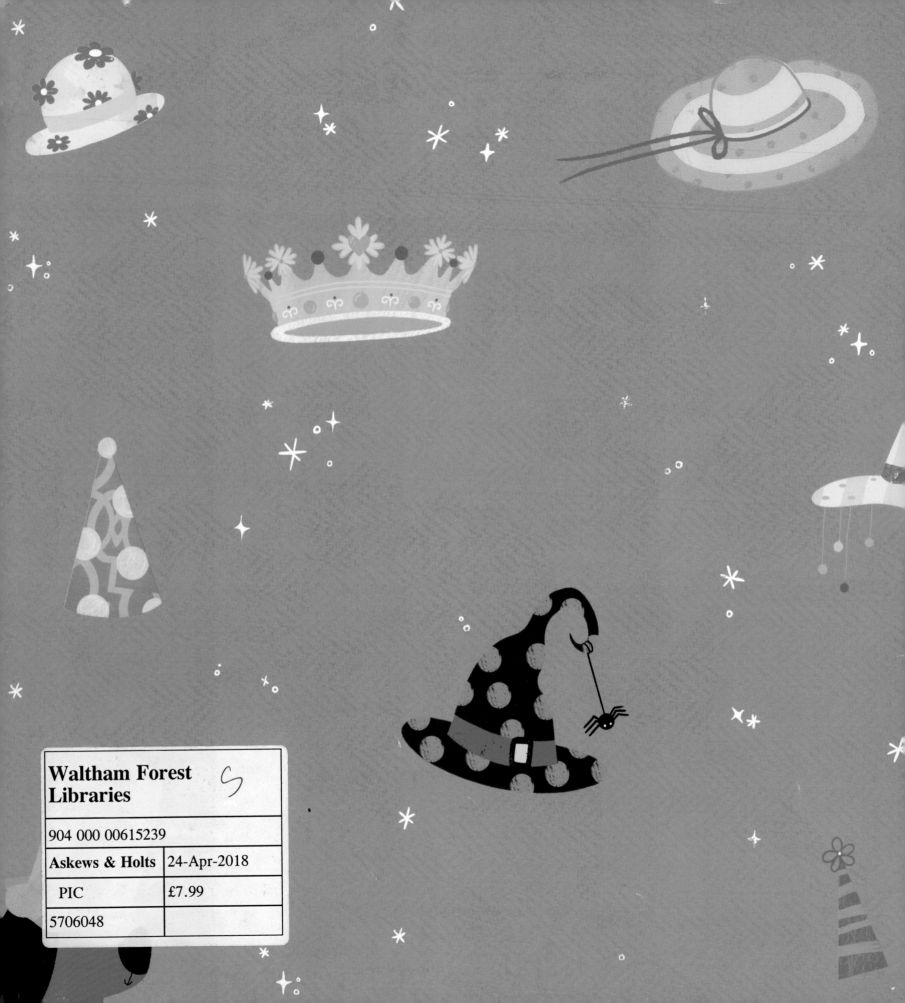

And Hettie wore them **all**.

One day, Hettie was fishing in her usual spot
on the ice when up popped Puffin.

"I need a **hat**," he said.

Hettie opened her bag, "I'll share my **lollies**, my **dollies**, my **books** and my **brollies**, my **flippers** and my **slippers** and I'll **even** share my **kippers**...

...but I'll **never, ever** share my HATS," she said.

Suddenly, Puffin felt hungry and he forgot all about the hats.

"I'll take the kippers," he said, and off he went.

Hettie put down her fishing rod.

It's time to change my hat, she thought.

She tried lace hats,

space hats, some in your face hats,

mop hats, flop hats, even over the top hats and she was just about to make her decision when...

"I need a hat," said Puffin.

Hettie shook her head. "Listen, Puffin," she said.

"I'll share my lollies, my dollies, my books and my brollies, my flippers and my slippers and you know I share my kippers, but

I'll never, ever share my HATS!"

Suddenly, Puffin's feet felt cold and he forgot all about the hats.

"I'll take the slippers," he said, and off he went.

Fishing can be boring and Hettie closed her eyes;

soon she was floating through **the hatmosphere.**

I've never seen so many hats, she thought.

There were...

...pirate hats, jester hats, pork pie and sou'wester hats,

cork hats, crown hats, witches and clown hats.

Then...

"**Wake up**," said Puffin,

"I need a hat."

Hettie growled, "I... don't... share... **hats!**"

"How about swapsies then?" asked Puffin, and he opened his backpack. "I'll swap... a **gnome?**"

"**No!**"

"A comb?"

"**NO!**"

"A dog with a bone?"

"NO!"

"**Yes!**" said Hettie,

"I need a scarf! Scarves look **splendid** with hats."

"And hats look **super** with scarves,"

said Puffin. Hettie had a thought...

"Sharing my hats might not be **SO** bad. Here," she said,
and handed Puffin the **handsomest** of hats. Puffin was delighted.

"I've got plenty of scarves," he said.

"I've got **long** scarves, **short** scarves, **knitted** and **bought** scarves, **stripy** scarves, **patchy** scarves, **soft** and **scratchy** scarves."

And **together...**

...they wore them all.

The End

Not My Hats!

An original concept by author Tracy Gunaratnam

© Tracy Gunaratnam

Illustrated by Alea Marley

MAVERICK ARTS PUBLISHING LTD

Studio 3A, City Business Centre, 6 Brighton Road, Horsham, West Sussex, RH13 5BB

© Maverick Arts Publishing Limited   +44 (0)1403 256941

Published March 2018

A CIP catalogue record for this book is available at the British Library.

ISBN 978-1-84886-324-8

Maverick
arts publishing

www.maverickbooks.co.uk

Waltham Forest Libraries C

Please return this item by the last date stamped. The loan may be renewed unless required by another customer.

10/2019		

Need to renew your books?
http://www.walthamforest.gov.uk/libraries or
Dial 0333 370 4700 for Callpoint – our 24/7 automated telephone renewal
line. You will need your library card number and your PIN. If you do not
know your PIN, contact your local library.